Plum Magic

Written by Margaret Nash
Illustrated by Julie Park

Rosie wanted to play with Sam.
But he was at Carlo's house.
Rosie was cross.
Sam was always with Carlo now.

She went over to Carlo's house.
She could see Carlo and Sam in the garden but
they couldn't see her. They were juggling.
Sam couldn't do it and he and Carlo were laughing.

Rosie picked up a ball.
Sam and Carlo were still
laughing and they still
didn't see her.
She picked up another ball.
Sam and Carlo still didn't see her.

Suddenly, Sam shouted, 'Two balls are missing!'
'Oh no!' said Carlo. 'They belong to my dad.
He'll go mad.'

Rosie climbed the plum tree.
She threw a ball at Sam and hit him hard.
'Ouch!' yelled Sam.
She threw another ball and hit Carlo hard.
'Ouch!' yelled Carlo.

Suddenly, Sam saw her.
Rosie laughed and
threw some plums at him.
'Ouch!' yelled Sam.

'Stop it, Rosie!'
shouted Carlo.
'My dad will go mad.
He wants the plums to
make a plum pie.'

Rosie threw some plums into
the garden next door.
'Stop it, Rosie!' shouted Carlo.
'The man next door will go mad.'
'Who's the man next door?' asked Rosie.

'I'm the man next door,' said a man, crossly.
'I'm Mr Pepper.'
Mr Pepper picked up a plum.
'Here,' he said to Carlo, 'take this.'
He picked up another plum and another plum.
He gave them all to Carlo.

'I'm sorry,' said Rosie to
Mr Pepper.

But Mr Pepper just
looked at her crossly,
and went back into his house.

Then The Great Lorenzo came into the garden.
Carlo said to Rosie, 'Here comes my dad.
He'll go mad when he sees you!'

Lorenzo looked up in the tree.
'Did you throw the plums down, Rosie?'
he asked.
'Y. . . Y. . . Yes,' said Rosie.

'Throw down some more, please,'
said Lorenzo, laughing.
Rosie threw down some more plums and
Lorenzo picked them all up.
Then he said to Rosie,
'Say, Izzie Whizzie, Plum Pie!'

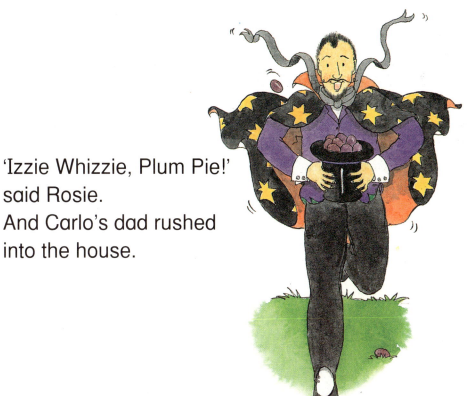

'Izzie Whizzie, Plum Pie!'
said Rosie.
And Carlo's dad rushed
into the house.

Rosie looked down at Carlo.
'Is your dad mad?'
she asked.

Lorenzo came back with
an enormous plum pie.

'That was quick,' said Sam.
'It's magic!' said Rosie, and
she climbed down from the tree.

They all ate some plum pie.
'It's great,' said Sam and Rosie, and
they all ate some more.

Carlo wanted a drink.

Lorenzo said,
'Izzie Whizzie,
in a wink.
Here's some magic
orange drink.'

He put some into Rosie's glass.
He put some into Carlo's glass.
He put some into Sam's glass.

He put some in the bird-bath and
he watered the flowers.

Still the jug was full.

'I wish the pie dish was still full,' said Sam.
'Say, Izzie Whizzie, Plum Pie!' said Lorenzo.
'Izzie Whizzie, Plum Pie!' shouted Sam,
and Lorenzo rushed into the house again.

He came back with another
enormous plum pie and
they ate it all up.
'Say, Izzie Whizzie, Plum Pie again,'
said Lorenzo.
'Izzie Whizzie, Plum Pie again,'
shouted Carlo.
'Oh no! No more plum pie, please,'
said Rosie, 'I'm full.'

Izzie Whizzie

Lorenzo went into the house, and came back with another enormous plum pie.
'I'm full too,' said Sam.
'I'm not,' said Carlo.

'It's not for you,' said Lorenzo.
'It's for Mr Pepper.'
'Can I give it to him, please?' asked Rosie.
'Yes, you can,' said Lorenzo.

'Can I come with you, Rosie?' asked Sam.
'Yes!' said Rosie. 'Let's go!'